SACRAMENTO PUBLIC LIBRARY
828 "I" STREET
SACRAMENTO, CA 95814
2/2010

D0463269

Dear Vampa

Written and illustrated by Ross Collins

KATHERINE TEGEN BOOKS
An Imprint of HarperCollins Publishers

Dear Vampa
Copyright © 2009 by Ross Collins
Manufactured in China.
All rights reserved. No part of this book may be used or reproduced in any manner
whatsoever without written permission except in the case of brief quotations embodied in
critical articles and reviews. For information address HarperCollins Children's Books, a division
of HarperCollins Publishers, 10 East 53rd Street, New York, NY 10022.
www.harpercollinschildrens.com

Library of Congress Cataloging-in-Publication Data
Collins, Ross.
Dear Vampa / written and illustrated by Ross Collins. — 1st ed.
p. cm.
Summary: A young vampire writes a letter to his grandfather bemoaning his new neighbors.
ISBN 978-0-06-135534-9 (trade bdg.)
[1. Vampires—Fiction. 2. Neighbors—Fiction. 3. Letters—Fiction. 4. Humorous stories.] I. Title.
PZ7.C6836De 2009   [E]—dc22   2008022631   CIP   AC

Typography by Rachel Zegar
09 10 11 12 13 SCP 10 9 8 7 6 5 4 3 2 1
❖
First Edition

For Eunice

To: Vampa
   The Ruined Abbey
   Lugosi Lane
   Transylvania

From: Bram Pire
   66 Nostfer Avenue
   Harkerville
   Pennsylvania

Dear Vampa,

Sorry for not writing for so long, but we've been having some trouble with our new neighbors.

They are called the Wolfsons.

They moved in three months ago
with an **awful** lot of weird stuff.

They invited us over for a "housewarming."

There was **nothing** to drink at all.

the Wolfsons stay up **all** day long.

We haven't had **any** sleep in weeks.

And then **they** had the nerve to complain when Mom had her friends over.

They have a bizarre fondness for sunshine.
Mom says it's disgusting.

The Wolfsons tend to lock their windows every night. It's **SO** inconsiderate.

Last month they invited us
to a Halloween party.

It wasn't much fun.

Their unpleasant pet
didn't seem to warm to us.

And they didn't seem to like Cuddles either.

Things came to a head on Wednesday.

We all went out for our evening flutter,
and the Wolfsons shot us out of the sky.

Dad says he has had enough.
He used some **very** bad words.

As I write, we are moving out. We are coming back to Transylvania to stay with you for a while.

Mom asks if you can get the guest crypt ready for us.

Hope this finds you unwell. All my love to Vampma.

Lovebites,

Bram x x x

"It's a pity the fires are moving, dear."

"It's so hard to find good neighbors."